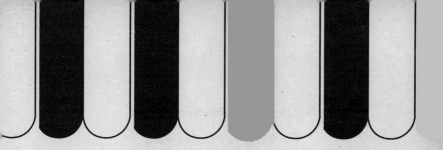

MR. POTTER'S PET

DICK KING-SMITH

ILLUSTRATED BY MARK TEAGUE

HYPERION PAPERBACKS FOR CHILDREN

New York

First Hyperion Paperback edition 1997

Text ©1996 by Dick King-Smith.
Illustrations © 1996 by Mark Teague.

A hardcover edition of *Mr. Potter's Pet* is available from Hyperion
Books for Children.

Printed in the United States of America.

1 3 5 7 9 10 8 6 4 2

Library of Congress Cataloging-in-Publication Data
King-Smith, Dick
Mr. Potter's pet / Dick King-Smith—1st ed.
p.   cm.
Summary: Mr. Potter's boring life changes considerably after buying an
unusual mynah bird.
ISBN:0-7868-1206-0   (paperback)
[1. Pets—Fiction. 2. Mynahs—Fiction. 3. Friendship—Fiction.]
I. Title.
PZ7.K5893Mr   1996
[Fic]—dc20   95-4824

The artwork for this book is prepared using ink.

The text for this book is set in 14-point Souvenir.

MR. POTTER'S PET

CHAPTER 1

Ever since he was a small boy, Mr. Potter had had a problem. It was not a medical problem, for he enjoyed excellent health. Nor was it a matter of money, for he had never felt the lack of it. Nor did he ever fall out with the neighbors or fall afoul of the law.

What Mr. Potter suffered from was an addiction.

Not to cigarettes—he didn't smoke; nor to alcohol—he didn't drink; nor to food—for though he had a good appetite, he was not greedy. Mr. Potter's addiction was not at all a usual one, and I doubt you would ever guess what it was. So I'll tell you.

Mr. Potter had never been able to stop himself from looking into the windows of pet shops.

First as a boy, then as a youth, and finally as an adult—for he continued to live at home with his parents—he would stand and gaze, year in, year out, and wish and wish that someday he might have a pet of his own. But never once did he enter a pet shop, for his mother and father, who did not like animals, had forbidden him to do so. Then, on Mr. Potter's fiftieth birthday, Fate took a hand.

To celebrate the occasion there was a choice of canned crab or pork pie for tea. Mr. Potter chose the pork pie, and it was fortunate he did so, for his mother and father agreed that something tasted ever so funny about the canned crab.

Twenty-four hours later, Mr. Potter was an orphan.

On the way home from his parents' funeral it just so happened that Mr. Potter had to pass his local pet shop. As he had always done, over the years, he stopped and stood and gazed into the window, at the puppies and kittens, at the rabbits and guinea pigs, at the parakeets and canaries. "If only I could have a pet of my own," he said wistfully, as he had always said, over the years.

Then it suddenly dawned on him. He could!

Who was to stop him? Thanks to the canned crab, no one.

Thanks to the canned crab, he need no longer simply stand and stare hopelessly at the window. He could go in! He could go in and buy himself a pet, any sort of pet—whatever he fancied!

As a small boy he'd always wanted a white mouse. As he grew, so did the animals he dreamed of owning—a gerbil, a hamster, a guinea pig, a rabbit—until when grown-up he thought how nice it would be to have a cat or a dog. But since he had never been allowed inside a pet shop, Mr. Potter had never had to make a choice. Now, suddenly, he could!

He pushed open the door.

"Shut that door!" cried a loud angry voice as Mr. Potter entered the shop, and he hastened to obey. He was accustomed always to do as he was told. But I must say, he thought, that shopkeeper is a very rude fellow. How does he expect to run a successful business if he shouts at his customers in that way?

However, when Mr. Potter turned around he thought that the shopkeeper looked like a polite sort of person, who smiled and said in quite a different tone, "Good morning, sir. What can I do for you?"

"Well," said Mr. Potter, "I want to buy a pet."

"For a grandchild perhaps?" asked the shopkeeper.

"No. For myself."

"What sort of pet?"

Mr. Potter turned to look at the cages ranged along the walls.

"I don't know," he said, to which the reply was, "Silly fool!"

Mr. Potter was a mild-mannered man who had never been known to say "boo" to a goose. For all of his fifty years he had done exactly as he was told, by his teachers at school and by his late mother and father at home. Which is why he had shut the door of the pet shop even though it seemed to him that the shopkeeper could well have said "please." But now to be called a silly fool by a perfect stranger was a bit much.

He took off his spectacles so as not to have to meet the shopkeeper's eye and polished them vigorously with his handkerchief.

"Just because I haven't yet made my mind up what sort of pet I want," Mr. Potter said rather nervously, "I really don't think you have any right to call me that."

The shopkeeper smiled.

"Call you what?" he asked, and, as if in answer, the different voice said, "Silly fool!"

Putting his spectacles on again, Mr. Potter saw that the speaker was sitting in a large cage hanging just above the shopkeeper's head. It was a bird the size of a dove, glossy black in color save for a white bar on each wing, with yellow feet and wattles, and a stout orange-red bill.

"I'm sorry," said the shopkeeper. "You're not the first person to complain about his language, not by a long shot. He's the rudest bird in the world, he is."

"What is he?" asked Mr. Potter.

"He's a mynah," said the shopkeeper. "A greater Indian hill mynah, to give him his proper title. They live in the forests of the hilly parts of India. Wonderful mimics they are, better than any parrot, and he's as good a one as I've ever heard, but he never says a civil word to anyone."

"Shut your face!" said the mynah.

"See what I mean?" said the shopkeeper. "No wonder I haven't been able to sell him. Now then, sir, perhaps I can help you choose a pet of some sort. Do you see anything you fancy?"

Mr. Potter pottered round the shop, looking at all the different animals that were for sale. All the time he kept half an eye on the mynah, waiting to hear what it would say next, but it remained silent.

Mr. Potter completed his tour of the shop and stood looking up at the bird.

"How much?" he asked.

"The mynah?" asked the shopkeeper.

"Yes," said Mr. Potter.

"Mind your own business," said the mynah.

"Two hundred fifty dollars," said the shopkeeper. "Which is a fair price, I assure you."

"Rubbish!" said the mynah.

"In fact," said the shopkeeper, "for two hundred fifty dollars I'll throw in the cage as well."

"Done!" said Mr. Potter.

"Silly fool!" said the mynah.

CHAPTER 2

At home Mr. Potter hung the cage in his parents' bedroom.

"This is *your* room from now on," he said to the mynah.

The bird turned its head this way and that, surveying its new quarters critically, first with one large liquid eye and then with the other.

"Well," said Mr. Potter. "How d'you like it?"

For its answer the mynah made a rude noise.

"That's not very polite," said Mr. Potter. "I ask you a civil question and I expect a civil answer. What do you think of your room?"

"It's a dump," said the mynah.

Mr. Potter shook his head and sighed. He could

see that he would have to educate the bird to say nice things instead of nasty ones. If he was always polite to it, surely it would learn by example?

"Pardon me for asking," he said, "but what is your name?"

"Mind your own business," said the mynah.

Mr. Potter smiled bravely.

"My name's Potter," he said.

The mynah laughed loudly. It was not a nice laugh.

"Can you say that? Potter . . . Potter . . . Potter."

"Ah, shut up!" said the mynah.

Mr. Potter picked up the telephone that stood beside his late parents' bed and dialed the number of the pet shop.

"Hello," he said. "I bought a mynah bird from you today."

"I'm sorry, sir," said the shopkeeper hastily, "but I can't possibly take him back. I've already paid your check into the bank."

"No, no," said Mr. Potter. "That's not why I'm calling. I simply forgot to ask you if he has a name."

"I called him a good many names," said the shopkeeper dryly, "and so will you, I expect."

Mr. Potter put down the receiver.

"That was the man at the pet shop," he said.

"Stupid old twit," said the mynah.

"Oh, I don't know. He seemed a nice chap."

"Rubbish!"

Mr. Potter began to feel that he had made a bad bargain. He had paid a great deal of money for this, his very first pet, attracted by its ability to speak as clearly as any human. Now, it seemed, he was condemned to putting up with its everlasting rudeness. If only it would say something reasonable. He tried again.

"Tell me, what would you like me to call you?" he said.

"Suit yourself," the bird said and turned its back on him.

Mr. Potter considered what name you could give a bad-tempered, bad-mannered greater Indian hill mynah, and that brought into his mind the greatest of Indian hills—well, more than that, the highest mountain in the world.

"How about 'Everest?'" he asked.

He waited for the mynah to say "shut up" or "silly fool" or "stupid old twit," but it simply said, "OK."

The tone of its voice was dispirited, as though it

didn't much care what it was called, and a sudden thought struck Mr. Potter. Was the bird simply unhappy? Was this why it was always so surly?

"Look, Everest," he said, "you've got plenty of good food—mealworms and a special mynah mixture that I bought from the pet shop—and some fresh fruit to peck at and clean water to drink and a handsome cage. What more do you want?"

"Use your brains," said Everest and, turning around, he began to hammer with his stout beak at the cage door.

He wants to come out, thought Mr. Potter.

"You want to come out?" he said.

"You got it, Potter," said Everest.

So surprised was Mr. Potter to be addressed by name that without further thought he reached up and unlatched the door of the cage.

The mynah hopped out and down onto his new owner's shoulder.

Mr. Potter could see out of the corner of his eye that strong orange-red bill, and it looked very sharp. He stood stock-still, expecting to be rewarded with a vicious peck from this grumpy bird.

Then to his great surprise he felt instead the gentlest of tugs at the lobe of his ear and heard the voice of his pet, sounding quite different from its usual harsh tones.

"Thanks, Potter," said Everest softly. "You're a pal."

Mr. Potter positively beamed with pleasure. Living at home under the thumbs of his mother and father, he had never in all his fifty years made any friends. Now at last, it seemed, he had one! And he had found the reason for Everest's constant rudeness. All the bird wanted was a little bit of freedom, an occasional outing from the confines of his cage, a short flight around the room perhaps. No harm in that; he couldn't escape—the window was closed. Wasn't it?

Mr. Potter turned his head and caught his breath. The top part of the old-fashioned sash window was a little way open, six inches maybe.

"Everest," he said.

"Yes, Potter?"

"How about popping back into your cage for a moment? There's something I've forgotten to do."

"So I see," said the mynah, and he jumped off Mr. Potter's shoulder and flew onto the top of the window frame.

"For a moment Everest perched there, turning his head for one last backward look.

"Nice knowing you, Potter," he said and was gone.

CHAPTER 3

All that evening Mr. Potter searched for his pet. He searched his own garden and looked into the gardens of his neighbors and walked all around the nearby park, crying, "Everest! Everest! Everest!" People he met looked at him askance. Those who knew him by sight thought he had become deranged by the sudden deaths of his mother and father. Those who didn't thought he was drunk.

"Everest! Everest! Where on earth are you?" he called, and an earnest-looking schoolboy took the question seriously and replied, "In the Himalayas. On the border between Nepal and Tibet." But of the mynah there was neither sight nor sound.

Darkness fell and Mr. Potter went to bed and slept badly. His pet was lost. He still had the cage of course, he could go to the pet shop and buy some other bird, but that would be cold comfort. Nothing could replace Everest, his first and only friend.

Nonetheless he got up very early in the morning and walked to the pet shop, hoping against hope that the mynah would be sitting outside its closed door, like a homing pigeon waiting to be let into its loft. But of course it wasn't.

Mr. Potter trudged despondently home again. After breakfast, he thought, I'll ring the police and I'll put advertisements everywhere and I'll offer a reward. But even if anyone saw him, how could they catch him? And supposing someone did and I got Everest back, the bird would have to be caged forever. Which is exactly what he hated and why he was so grumpy. At least now he's free, Mr. Potter said to himself, free as a bird. So one of us is happy.

He put aside the thought of breakfast and went

upstairs, nerving himself to face the empty room, the empty cage. He opened the door.

"Morning, Potter," said a muffled voice, and there, in his cage, on his perch, was the mynah with a mouthful of mealworms.

Mr. Potter's first impulse was to rush forward and close the window. If I can manage to do that, he thought, then even if I'm not quick enough to shut the door of the cage, at least he won't be able to get out of the room. But before he could move, Everest swallowed the mealworms, hopped out of the cage, and perched on the back of a chair.

"Shut the window, Potter," he said. "There's an awful draft."

Stunned, Mr. Potter obeyed.

"You're back!" he said hoarsely.

"Looks like it," said Everest.

"But . . . but why?"

"Hungry. And cold. Too many cats about anyway. You haven't got one, I hope?"

"No, no, you're the first pet I've ever had."

"Pet, eh? That's a bit patronizing."

"Oh, sorry. The first friend, I meant to say, Everest," said Mr. Potter.

"That's better," said the mynah.

He began to preen himself, stretching his wings and settling his feathers.

"Potter," said Everest, "you've never had a girl-friend either?"

Peggy Flower, thought Mr. Potter! The only girl-friend I ever had. At least that's how I thought of her, though I never told her how I felt. She was small and rather plump with fair hair; I can see her now. Though we were the same age, we were in different classes, but I would watch her in the play-ground, skipping about with some of the other girls, and she smiled at me, once.

"Penny for your thoughts, Potter," said Everest, his head cocked to one side.

A silly idea came into Mr. Potter's mind, which was that when the mynah looked at him like that, the bird could actually read his thoughts, never mind offering a penny for them.

"I did have a girlfriend, Everest," he said.

"Turned you down, did she?" said the mynah.

"No."

"Why didn't you marry her, then?"

"We were only ten," said Mr. Potter. "She moved away. I've never seen her since."

"About this cage, Potter," Everest said.

"Yes?"

"OK for sleeping in. OK for eating in. But in the future, let's leave the door open. OK?"

"You mean, you want to be free to fly about the house?" said Mr. Potter.

"Sure," said Everest. "No problem there, is there?"

A great many problems, thought Mr. Potter. He pictured the equestrian statue in the middle of the park, liberally bespattered with pigeon droppings, and imagined the state in which his house would very shortly be. But how should he put it to Everest?

At that moment the mynah finished his preening and, raising his tail, deposited a large squidgy white mess on the bedroom carpet.

"That's better," he said.

"Well, actually," said Mr. Potter, "it's not."

"Oh, sorry, Potter," said Everest. "I didn't think. Not used to being out of a cage. Where do you want me to do it?"

Mr. Potter hesitated. Outside in the garden, I suppose, he thought. But then Everest might fly away again.

"Outside in the garden?" said Everest.

"But . . . ,"said Mr. Potter.

"Worry not, pal," said Everest, flying up onto his shoulder. "East, west, home's best. But supposing it's snowing or blowing a gale or raining cats and dogs? Where do you do it, Potter?"

Dazedly Mr. Potter walked to the bathroom with its old-fashioned claw-footed bath and its antiquated plumbing fixtures—a high tank and dangling chain—and pointed to the toilet bowl.

"In there?" asked Everest.

"Yes," said Mr. Potter, "and then you can get rid of it." He pulled the handle.

Head cocked, the mynah watched the water flushing away.

"Neat," he said.

"You could, um, manage could you?" said Mr. Potter.

"No major problem there," said Everest. "Not even a mynah one. But I'm all right at the moment, thanks." And once again he nibbled at the lobe of Mr. Potter's ear.

Mr. Potter suddenly felt not merely very happy but very hungry.

"Come on, Everest," he said. "I haven't had any breakfast yet, and I daresay you wouldn't mind another beakful."

In the kitchen Mr. Potter got out the frying pan and cooked himself a huge fatty breakfast, just the kind his mother had never given him—bacon and eggs and mushrooms and baked beans and black pudding and a big slice of fried bread. And he sat himself down at the head of the table, where his father had always sat, with his elbows on the table, which his mother had never allowed. He had taken off his jacket and his tie, something that neither of his parents would ever have permitted, and he sat there in his shirtsleeves, shoveling the food in like a greedy schoolboy while the grease ran down his chin and the mynah stood on the table, nibbling at a biscuit and watching attentively.

Mr. Potter cut himself another thick slice of bread and wiped all around his greasy plate. He swallowed the last mouthful and let out a loud satisfied belch.

"Nice one, Potter," said Everest.

"Oh dear," said Mr. Potter. "I beg your pardon. I was forgetting my manners."

"Worry not, pal," said Everest. "That was the mother and father of a meal you put away. Do you always eat like that?"

"Well, no," said Mr. Potter. "My mother and father, you see, would not have approved. They ate very sparingly."

But, in the end, not wisely, he thought.

"Fallen off their perches, have they?" said Everest.

"Sorry?"

"Shot their bolt? Had their chips? Turned their toes up? Popped their clogs? Died?"

"Yes, very recently. Last week, in fact."

"And you've lived with them here? All your life?"

"Yes."

Everest let out a low whistle of amazement.

"Weird, Potter," he said. "Really weird. I flew the nest the moment I got my flight feathers."

"They didn't want me to go," said Mr. Potter.

They didn't let me do anything I wanted to, he thought.

"You must miss 'em," said the mynah.

"Oh yes," said Mr. Potter absently, taking a long noisy drink of the strong Indian tea that his parents, preferring weak China, and never kept.

"You'll be lonely," said Everest.

"Not now," said Mr. Potter. "Not now I've got you for a friend."

Everest cast a critical eye around the kitchen. He saw the ants crawling around the floor, the spiderwebs in the corners of the ceiling, the smeary windows, the stack of dishes in the sink, the dirty dishcloths, the dust everywhere.

"That's all very well, Potter," he said. "But what you need is someone to help you keep house."

CHAPTER 4

Oh, no," said Mr. Potter.

"What's the matter?" said Everest. "Can't afford it?"

"It isn't that," said Mr. Potter, and indeed it wasn't, for thanks to that can of crab, he was now so well off that he had even been able to give up the job that had bored him stiff for thirty years.

But to have a strange person living in my house, he thought—I couldn't bear that. People had always made him feel shy.

"Oh, no," he said. "I'll manage."

"We'll see," said Everest.

And over the coming weeks they saw.

Never before had Mr. Potter realized the meaning of housework. Now he found it never ending. Quite apart from tidying the place up and trying to keep it clean, there was the shopping and the cooking and the washing and the ironing and the mending. There was silver to be polished and brass to be burnished and windows to be cleaned—the list was endless. So it was that in due course an advertisement appeared in the local newspaper:

> Respectable bachelor, 50, nonsmoker, sober, simple tastes, requires live-in housekeeper. Generous wages, holidays for suitable applicant. Own comfortable quarters. Apply Mr. Peter Potter, The Laurels, Greenfield Avenue.

The very next morning there was a loud knock at the door.

Mr. Potter paled.

"Oh, Everest," he said. "What if they're not suitable?"

"Leave that to me," said Everest. "You give me a sign and I'll do the rest."

"What sort of sign?"

"Scratch your bald spot."

The moment he opened the door, Mr. Potter knew he was not going to like the large jolly woman who thrust out a hand that gripped his own like a vise.

"We'll soon have this place to rights," she boomed as Mr. Potter showed her around. "I can see we're going to get on like a house on fire, ha, ha, not a happy choice of words, eh?"

Not a happy choice of housekeeper, thought Mr. Potter, and he looked widely around for Everest, but the mynah was nowhere to be seen.

"I'll start next week then, Mr. Potter," said the large jolly woman.

Oh, what shall I do? thought Mr. Potter. What can I say? Where's Everest? He scratched his bald spot like mad.

"That's agreed then," said the woman, and Mr. Potter opened his mouth to say he knew not what. At that instant he heard the sound of his own voice, coming somewhere just behind his head.

"No, it isn't," said his voice. "I wouldn't employ

you if you were the last person on earth. Now get lost."

As the front door banged furiously behind the outraged woman, Everest emerged from his hiding place.

"Neat, eh, Potter?" he said in his normal harsh tones.

"You were brilliant," said Mr. Potter. "Just when I thought she had me cornered."

"Worry not, pal," said Everest. "We need to find the right person. Better luck next time, maybe."

The next applicant arrived that afternoon. In contrast to the first one, she was soft-spoken and daintily dressed, and her hand, as Mr. Potter greeted her, felt soft and lingered in his long enough to make him uncomfortable. Everything about her was ladylike. Her voice was carefully genteel, and she constantly fluttered her eyelashes and smiled roguishly at Mr. Potter.

After their tour of the house she stood very close to him in the sitting room, in front of the bookcase in which Everest was crouching. The sight of that ladylike bottom was too much for the mynah.

"Oh! Mr. Potter!" squealed the would-be housekeeper happily. "You are naughty!"

"Naughty?" said Mr. Potter, puzzled.

"Pinching a girl's sit-upon! I can see we're going to have lots of fun!"

Once again Mr. Potter scratched his bald spot with a will, and once again as he prepared to reply, he heard his own voice.

"Not on your nellie!" it said. "Go and make sheep's eyes at someone else."

"I couldn't resist it," said Everest when the front door had banged again. "Just a couple of little tweaks, that's all."

Mr. Potter mopped his eyes.

"Oh dear!" he said. "What a laugh! But I'm still no nearer to getting a housekeeper."

The telephone rang.

"Yes?" said Mr. Potter. "Yes, that's right. No, the position isn't filled. This evening at seven? Yes, that's quite convenient. Good-bye." He turned to the mynah.

"She sounded all right," he said.

"Third time lucky?" said Everest.

CHAPTER 5

As seven o'clock approached, Mr. Potter found himself becoming increasingly nervous. The way that Everest had disposed of the first two applicants was all very well, but Mr. Potter did hope that this time he would not have to call upon the bird for help.

It was not in his nature to be rude or unkind to people, and already he felt guilty that those two women had been so treated.

"Everest," he said.

"Yes, Potter?"

"If this one's no good, d'you think you could let her off a bit more lightly? Be a bit more polite, I mean?"

The mynah put his head to one side.

"Feeling guilty, huh?" he said.

"Yes."

"Suit yourself," said Everest. "In fact, why not tell her yourself? If you don't like the look of her, all you have to do is say, 'I will let you know my decision later.'"

"All right," said Mr. Potter.

He looked at his watch.

"Do you need to go outside?" he asked.

"Too dark," said Everest. "Owls and pussycats out there. I'll pop up to the bathroom."

"Better pull the handle," he said when he returned, and no sooner had Mr. Potter obeyed than there was a knock on the front door.

The first thing Mr. Potter noticed as he opened it was that this woman had a particularly nice smile.

She was middle-aged, of below-average height, and comfortably rounded, and her handshake was neither fierce nor flabby, but firm.

She had good things to say about the house and sensible suggestions to make as Mr. Potter showed

her around, and she seemed most understanding as he told her of the loss of his parents and of the problems that he now faced. Mr. Potter found that he was not at all shy with her. It was almost as though they were old friends.

"Shall I make a pot of tea?" he asked when they had finished their tour.

"Please," she said, "can't I make it for you?"

"No, no," said Mr. Potter, thinking how nice it would be to have his tea made and brought to him by this pleasant person.

"Indian or China?" he said.

"Indian, please," said the pleasant person. "And strong enough to stand the spoon up in!"

"Oh good!" said Mr. Potter. "That's the way I like it. By the way, I didn't catch your name."

"It's Margaret."

"I noticed a birdcage," said Margaret as they were sitting drinking their tea, "in that big bedroom that used to be your parents'."

"Ah yes," said Mr. Potter. "I should have told you. I do have a pet."

"Really?" said Margaret. "What sort?"

At that precise moment Everest, who had been listening outside the door, hopped into the room and straight up onto the arm of her chair.

"Oh!" she cried. "How lovely! A greater Indian hill mynah!" and she stretched out her hand and began to stroke Everest gently down the length of his glossy black back.

Any concerns that Mr. Potter had ever had about the wisdom of employing a housekeeper vanished at that instant, and at the same time he also knew beyond doubt that this was the person for the job.

"His name is Everest," he said. "You would be working for both of us."

Margaret smiled that nice smile.

"You don't recognize me, do you?" she asked.

Recognize her, thought Mr. Potter, why on earth should I? And in his puzzlement he raised a hand and scratched his bald spot. As he did so, he saw Everest watching him, head to one side.

"No!" he said loudly.

"You mean, you don't recognize me?"

"Oh, sorry," said Mr. Potter. "I was talking to Everest. I thought he might be going to say something."

"Is he a good talker?"

"Worry not, pal," said Everest to Mr. Potter. "I read you. Like a book."

Margaret almost dropped her teacup.

"What an absolutely amazing bird!" she said. "He doesn't just talk. He makes sense. What else does he say?"

"Anything you like, miss," said Everest, "so long as it's in plain English."

"And in plain English," said Mr. Potter, "the job is yours if you want it."

"Oh, I do," said Margaret, "and thank you. But I can see you're still wondering who I am, so I'd better put you out of your misery, Peter."

"How do you know my name?" asked Mr. Potter.

"It was in the advertisement, wasn't it? 'Can it be the same Peter Potter?' I asked myself. I've only just moved back to these parts, you see. I was working up north and I lost my job. So I thought I'd like to come back and look for a job in the town where I was born. And I'm so glad I did. But I haven't told you my surname, have I, Peter? It's Flower."

"Flower!" cried Mr. Potter, and now it was his turn to almost drop his cup. He stared at the figure sitting opposite him, small and rather plump with fair hair now peppered with gray, and suddenly he was watching Peggy Flower skipping about in the playground with some of the other girls as forty years vanished without a trace.

"But she wasn't called Margaret," he said.

"Oh yes, she was," said his new housekeeper. "Peggy for short."

CHAPTER 6

With the coming of Peggy Flower, life at the Laurels changed completely. After a couple of months, Mr. Potter had almost forgotten how dark and dingy the place had been all his life. Now there was bright fresh paint—his own handiwork, what's more—everywhere. Room by room, he had redecorated the entire house while Peggy reorganized it and Everest flew between them, carrying messages from one to the other.

"Peggy says, 'Do you want some coffee?'" he might say to the painter or, to the housekeeper, "Potter says, 'Isn't it lunchtime yet?'"

Mr. Potter now occupied his parents' old room.

"It's the nicest bedroom in the house, Peter,"

said Peggy, "as well as the biggest. I shall be perfectly happy in your old room, and, Everest, you could have the smaller of the spare rooms, couldn't you? It's handy for the bathroom and it overlooks the back garden. Not far for you to go, either way. Would that be OK?"

"Worry not, Peg," said Everest, and he treated her ear to a nibble.

Altogether the three of them were very content with one another's company. No thought crossed their minds that anything might happen to upset the even tenor of their days and ways. But it did.

One morning Peggy returned from shopping to find Mr. Potter in a right old state.

"Oh, I'm so glad you're back!" he cried as she came into the kitchen.

"Everest has had an accident! Look!" and there on the table lay the still body of Mr. Potter's pet.

"What happened?" asked his housekeeper.

"He flew upstairs to go to the bathroom," said Mr. Potter, "and after a while I thought, He's been gone a long time, and I went upstairs, and there he was on the floor. The lid of the toilet was down. It

must have fallen and hit him on the head. I think he's dead."

Peggy Flower picked up the mynah and held him in her hands.

"No he isn't," she said. "I can feel his heart beating," and quickly she emptied her shopping basket and laid Everest, wrapped in a dishcloth, in it.

"Off you go to the vet," she said to Mr. Potter, "and try not to worry. I'm sure he'll be all right."

"Will he be all right?" Mr. Potter anxiously asked the vet. "I think he's had a bang on the head."

"How did it happen?" asked the vet.

"I'm, er, not sure," said Mr. Potter. "I haven't been able to ask him, you see."

The vet raised his eyebrows.

"Answers questions, does he?" he said.

Mr. Potter smiled nervously. If he only knew, he thought. He watched as the vet carefully examined the mynah.

"Flew into a plate-glass window, I suppose, that's the usual thing," the vet said. "Stupid bird.

What's his name?"

"Everest," said Mr. Potter.

"Everest, eh!" said the vet with a grin. "Well, I tell you what, he's bumped his summit on the sum-mat! But I don't think he's cracked his skull, so we mustn't make mountains out of molehills, eh?"

At this point the mynah opened one eye.

"Oh, Everest!" cried Mr. Potter. "Speak to me!"

Everest opened the other eye.

"Say something—anything!"

"Who's a pretty boy then?" asked the vet.

Everest remained silent.

"He's lost for words," said the vet dryly. "But I can't find much wrong with him. Take him away and keep him warm—inside as well as out."

"Inside?" said Mr. Potter.

"Yes. Give him a drop of something, to help him to get over the shock. Brandy will do."

"A drop of brandy," said Mr. Potter when he arrived home.

"For you?" asked Peggy, producing a bottle from the pantry.

"No, for Everest."

"He's all right?"

"He's conscious."

"Has he spoken?"

"Not a word."

"And nor would you," said Everest weakly, "if you had a headache like mine."

Mr. Potter and Ms. Flower looked at each other over the shopping basket, and their eyes shone with relief and joy.

Carefully, Peggy filled a teaspoon.

"Now then, Everest," she said, "would you like

a little drink?" And as the mynah opened his beak to reply, she tipped the brandy down him.

"Nice?" asked Mr. Potter.

"Better?" asked Peggy.

"Yes," said Everest in a voice that was already a good deal stronger. "How about the other half?"

"We'll have one, too, shall we?" said Mr. Potter to his housekeeper and, to his pet, "Here's to a complete recovery. Your health, Everest!"

"Cheers!" said Peggy.

"Down the hatch!" said Everest.

"Now then," said Mr. Potter, "you have a good sleep and you'll wake up feeling a new bird."

For the rest of the day the Laurels was unnaturally quiet as Everest sat silent in his cage. Mr. Potter attended to the toilet lid, ensuring that it would not fall again, and Peggy went to the pet shop for fresh mealworms and to the greengrocer for Everest's favorite fruit, black grapes.

Tempted by these, the mynah ate a hearty supper and his spirits revived. When the others had finished, Mr. Potter, as always, offered to help with the washing up, and, as always, was told to go and sit down in his comfortable armchair.

In the kitchen Everest perched on the dish rack and watched the housekeeper at the sink.

"Why won't you let Potter help you?" he asked.

Peggy laughed.

"Because I'm paid to help him," she said.

Everest considered this.

"Suppose you were married to him," he said, "then he'd be expected to help you."

Despite herself, Ms. Flower blushed.

"Oh, get along with you!" she said, and flapped the dishcloth at him. Everest flew to the sitting room and perched on the arm of Mr. Potter's chair.

"You ever been married, Potter?" he asked.

"Oh, no," said Mr. Potter.

"Your mum and dad wouldn't let you, huh?"

It wasn't that, thought Mr. Potter, though it might have been.

"No," he said. "I just never met anyone I wanted to marry."

Except one person, he said to himself, and his face grew red.

Everest cocked his head to one side in that

mind-reading fashion and Mr. Potter took refuge behind his newspaper.

In the still of the night, Everest perched in his cage, thinking long and hard.

"It's the perfect match," he at last said softly. "They're just right for each other. But she can't very well make the first move. And he's too shy. There's only one way out. I'll have to fix it."

He lost no time about it.

The very next morning he flew in from the garden, where Mr. Potter was doing some weeding, to the kitchen, where Peggy was baking.

"Message from Potter," he said.

"What is it?" asked Peggy.

"He says—will you marry him?" said Everest, and off he went back to the garden.

"Message from Peggy," he said to Mr. Potter.

"What is it?"

"She says—will you marry her?" said Everest, and he flew away to the kitchen again.

"Well?" he asked.

"Oh yes!!" said Peggy.

Back went the mynah to the garden.

"Well?" he asked.

"Oh yes!!" said Mr. Potter.

"Well, don't just stand there, Potter," said Everest. "Get on with it."

As Mr. Potter walked dazedly up the garden path, he saw Peggy Flower looking at him out of the kitchen window. She was smiling at him just as she had in the playground, all those years ago.

As if in a dream, he made his way to the kitchen and went toward her, his muddy hands outstretched, and she took them in her floury ones, and they stood, speechless, smiling at each other.

"Come on, Potter," said a harsh voice from the doorway. "You may kiss the housekeeper."

So Mr. Potter did.

CHAPTER 7

Before long Everest began to regret his match-making.

So wrapped up in each other were the engaged couple that they paid much less attention to Mr. Potter's pet. Everest's beak was out of joint. "Pair of blooming lovebirds," he muttered sulkily. "Billing and cooing from morning till night. I might as well be stuffed for all the notice they take of me nowadays," and in a huff, he flew out and perched on the top of a tall tree.

In the garden below, Mr. Potter and Peggy sat side by side on a rustic seat, holding hands.

"Dearest," said Mr. Potter. "What would you like for a wedding present?"

"Another ring," said Peggy, for Mr. Potter had already bought her a handsome engagement ring. "A plain gold one. That's all I want."

"No, as well as that, I mean," said Mr. Potter. "There must be something you've always wanted, isn't there?"

"Funnily enough," said Peggy, "there is. Just like you, Peter, I've always longed for a pet of my own, but I could never have a dog, for instance, because I was always out at work."

"I'll buy you a puppy," said Mr. Potter.

"No, that's not what I would like."

"What then?"

Peggy whispered in Mr. Potter's ear.

"You're joking!" he said.

"No, I'm not."

"It may take ages to get one of those."

"I don't mind waiting."

"Right," said Mr. Potter. "I'll ring up that chap at the pet store straight away."

In fact it was not until after the wedding that Mrs. Potter's present arrived at the Laurels.

One day Mr. Potter came home carrying a cardboard box. Cautiously he opened the lid a little way and he and Peggy peaked in.

"Oh, isn't she lovely!" cried Mrs. Potter. "Thank you, Peter dear!" and she gave her new husband a kiss.

"Now then," he said. "Where's Everest?"

"Sitting up in his tree."

"Right, let's get everything fixed up."

So it was that, ten minutes later, Everest, hearing his name called, came flying through the kitchen window. He looked at the Potters and saw that they were both grinning broadly. He put his head to one side.

"What's up?" he said.

"Listen, Everest," said Mr. Potter. "Peggy and I just wanted to say we're sorry if we seem to have been neglecting you lately, what with the wedding and everything."

"Worry not, pal," said Everest flatly.

"But we do worry," said Mrs. Potter, "and I do hope that you won't object to my new pet."

"Your new pet?" said Everest. "Not a cat?"

"No, no," they said.

"Hop up on my shoulder, old chap," said Mr. Potter, "and we'll go up to your room."

"My room?" said Everest. "You've put some new animal in my room?"

"Yes, yes," they said, and they opened the door of Everest's little bedroom.

There, in his cage, was a bird the size of a dove, glossy black in color save for a white bar on each wing, with yellow feet and wattles, and a stout orange-red bill.

The Potters stood side by side before the cage.

"Meet Peggy's new pet," said Mr. Potter.

"My mynah," said Mrs. Potter.

Everest said nothing.

Instead he nibbled gently at Mr. Potter's ear.

Then he hopped across and nibbled at Mrs. Potter's ear.

Then he hopped back and fixed the newcomer with a long, slow stare.

Then he let out a long, low wolf whistle.

"She's beautiful, isn't she?" said Mrs. Potter.

"You said it," replied Everest.

"She doesn't say much," said Mr. Potter.

"She will," replied Everest.

"You'll teach her?"

"Worry not, Potter," said Everest. "I'll teach her a thing or two."

"Oh, Peter," sighed Mrs. Potter. "She's the nicest wedding present anyone ever had."

"I'm so glad you're pleased," said Mr. Potter.

"I certainly am," said Mrs. Potter.

"Me, too," said Mr. Potter's pet.